LUCY's

Journey to the Wild West

A TRUE STORY

By Charlotte Piepmeier

Illustrated by Sally Blakemore

Azro Press • Santa Fe, New Mexico • 2002

Lucy's Journey to the Wild West

ISBN 1-929115-07-5

Library of Congress Control Number: 2001096024

Azro Press • PMB 342 • 1704 Llano St B
Santa Fe, NM 87505

Designed by Marcy Heller
The text is set in 13 point Palatino
The cap initials are set in 60 point Curlz MT
The illustrations are water color.
Maps by Marcy Heller

Many thanks to Gibbs Smith Publisher for the biscochito recipe on page 33.
It is from the book *The Santa Fe School of Cooking*, by Susan Curtis.
Salt Lake City: Gibbs Smith, Publisher, 1995. Used with permission.

Lucy, a chocolate Labrador retriever, moves with her family from North Carolina to Santa Fe, New Mexico. Along the way she visits many interesting places. When she arrives in Santa Fe, she learns several lessons about living on the edge of a mountainous desert.

This book looks at the distress children feel about moving; the geography and history of the parts of the states they drive through; and the difficulties and rewards of settling into a new place.
Ages 5 - 12• Grades K - 6

Printed in Thailand

Published in

1 0 9 8 7 6 5 4 3 2

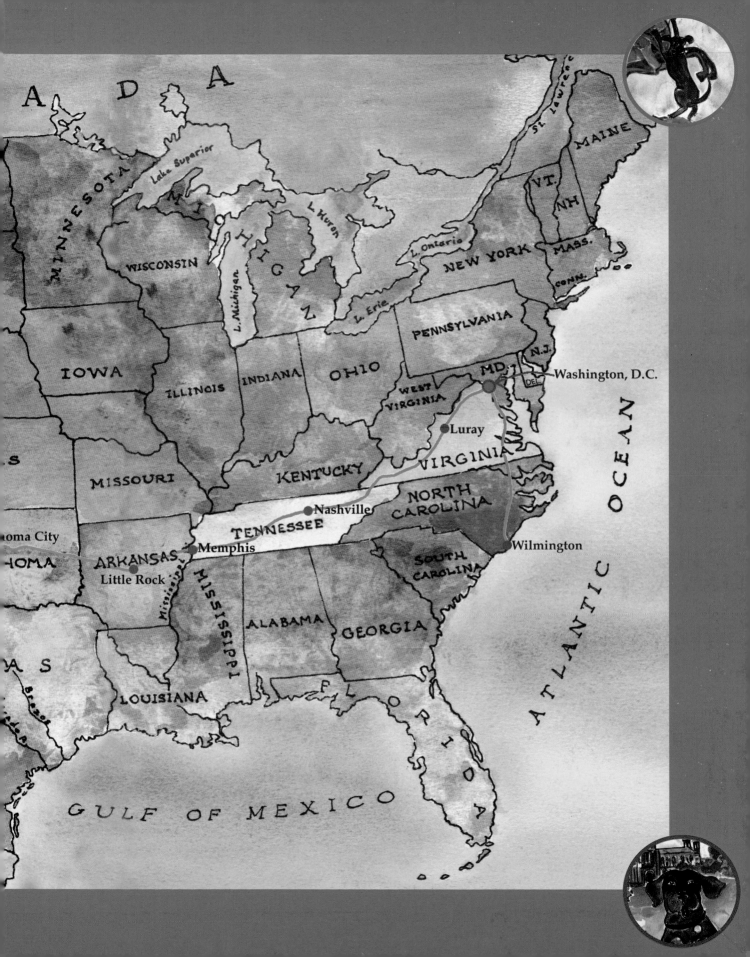

Contents

North Carolina

Wilmington

Lucy

is my name.

You probably think I'm a little girl. I'm a girl all right, but I'm not little—I'm big, and I'm a chocolate Labrador retriever.

Here's a picture of me as a little puppy in North Carolina.

North Carolina

I used to live on an inlet on the coast in North Carolina. We lived in a condominium. A condominium is an apartment building, but you own the apartment you live in.

We lived on the third floor of our building and used the elevator. You wouldn't believe the expressions of the people getting onto the elevator when they realized that a big dog (me) was on the elevator.

Floor 3

Floor 2

Floor 1

One day a little girl got on the elevator.

She was so cute I just had to give her a big, wet slurp right on the face. She took a huge step back, but then she giggled.

I think she liked it!

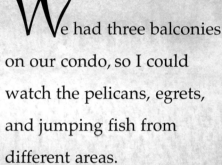

ZZZ-ZZZ-ZZZ-Z-ZZZ-ZZZ-Z

7 a.m.

9 a.m.

ZZZ-ZZZ-ZZZ-Z-ZZZ-ZZZ-Z

11 a.m.

1 p.m.

3 p.m.

ZZZ-ZZZ-ZZZ-Z-ZZZ-ZZZ-Z

5 p.m.

We had three balconies on our condo, so I could watch the pelicans, egrets, and jumping fish from different areas.

Watching all this activity kept me busy, so I took a lot of naps.

Most beach buildings are built on pilings. Pilings look like telephone poles driven into the ground. If a bad storm comes, the water goes beneath the house and the house stays dry. Thank goodness, we didn't have any big storms when I lived there.

3

Lots of fishing boats went right by our place, and I wagged my tail when the fishermen waved to me. When the big head boats came back in, they had all the fish they had caught on the trip hanging from big hooks. Sometimes I'd go down to the town dock to give them a friendly welcome bark.

Oh, the fish smells were so great! Ask any fisherman how good fish smell. I'd stand right by the fishermen's ice coolers, so I could get real good whiffs of the fish.

4

I loved walking and running on the beach and playing in the surf. My folks (Papa Pete and Mama C) liked to look for shells. I liked to hunt for critters like little sand crabs on the beach. Doesn't that sound like a perfect life?

You won't believe where my folks bathed me. We had a marina where the people in our building tied up their boats. So they took me down to the dock, hosed me off, and gave me a good bath.

But one day my folks told me that we were moving to New Mexico. I howled in protest. I loved it at the beach. My life was perfect.

My folks kept telling me how much I'd love New Mexico. They said how great it was, and that I'd find new dog friends there. Well, I didn't want any part of it. New Mexico was in the Wild West! I was perfectly happy living at the ocean.

I know Papa Pete and Mama C really love me. They take such good care of me. They give me good food

In spite of my protests, my folks started packing and crating. I didn't mind it so much when they packed away my shampoo, but when my big box of bones disappeared, I knew I was in trouble.

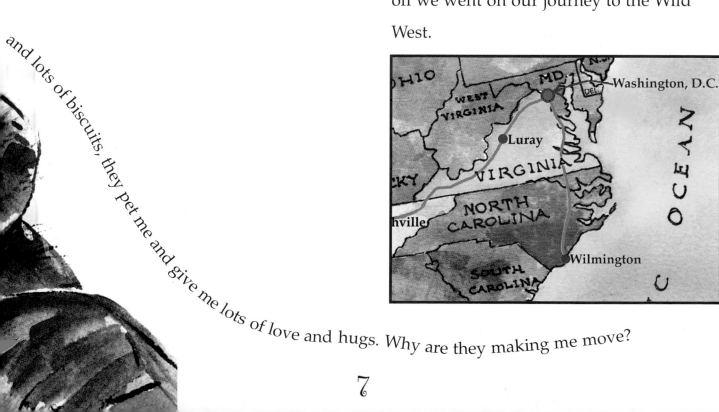

The moving day arrived, and I had to say good bye to my beloved home and all of my dog friends. At least, they put my dog bed and some of my toys in the back seat of the car, and off we went on our journey to the Wild West.

and lots of biscuits, they pet me and give me lots of love and hugs. Why are they making me move?

Washington, D.C., & through the Appalachians

The first day we went up to Washington, D.C., to see Brad. Brad is Papa Pete and Mama C's son, but he's like a brother to me. At least there's one good thing about this trip — I'll get to see my other two brothers, Craig and Steve, as we travel west.

Washington, D.C., is our nation's capital. Brad drove us around so we could see the Potomac River, the White House (where the President lives), and the huge government buildings.

Brad lives in a third floor apartment with no elevator. Do you realize how many steps that is? Every time I wanted to go out, I had no trouble going down the steps, but I was really panting going back up. I wasn't in shape for that. I decided I needed to start going to a gym and working out.

I particularly noticed one thing driving around D.C. Steps, steps, steps! Many buildings have numerous steps leading up to them. That makes all the buildings look so formidable.

Did you know that the National Zoo has two pandas from China? Does that mean if I talked to the pandas in doggy talk that they would speak to me in the Chinese language?

Another interesting sight was the number of equestrian (horse) statues in D.C. Our capital has more equestrian statues than any other city in our nation. I wonder what city has the most dog statues? I'd like to go there and check them out.

After a few days in D.C., we left for Aunt Ester's house in Tennessee. A good part of the day we were driving in the Shenandoah Valley between the Blue Ridge Mountains and the Allegheny Mountains of Virginia. We came to the Luray Caverns. It was a neat place to stop.

Further down the Blue Ridge Parkway we came to Natural Bridge. Can you imagine a limestone bridge that is 215 feet high and 90 feet long? That's as tall as a 15-story building! Now a highway goes on top of it.

The caverns have thousands of colored-stone formations called stalactites. In the Cathedral Room there is a Stalacpipe Organ, which uses specially tuned stalactites to produce music. I didn't get to hear the music but that was probably a good thing. High notes bother my ears, and I would have howled.

Our first president, George Washington, carved his initials in the bridge. You can still see them today if you look carefully.

That would be a loooooong look down from up there!

UTAH

IOWA

Pueblo

KANSAS

MISS

Trinidad

Raton

Oklahoma City

ARK

Santa Fe

OKLAHOMA

Little

IZONA

NEW MEXI

Just east of Nashville, Tennessee, we stopped at the Hermitage. It was the home of our nation's seventh president, Andrew Jackson. Jackson was considered the first president from the West because he was from the wilds of Tennessee. Now, I'm confused —Tennessee is not the West today!

The Hermitage had beautiful grounds, and the plants had new and different smells for me. It felt good to be out of the car running around.

Finally we arrived at Aunt Ester's house. Aunt Ester must have really liked me, because she put a little white fur rug under the baby grand piano, just for me. It was the perfect spot for a long nap. That is, it was the perfect spot until I jumped up suddenly. I banged my head on the piano and nearly knocked myself goofy. After that, I was a little more careful when I got up from under the piano.

The next day we were on the road again, this time to Memphis, Tennessee. My folks toured Elvis Presley's home, Graceland. They were quite impressed.

Apparently, Papa Pete had trouble leaving the cars until he discovered the jet airplane sitting on the lawn. Mama C almost couldn't get Papa Pete to leave.

Mama C liked looking at Elvis's costumes, awards, and the different videos about his life and career. She also talked about the jungle den. She said that it was dark, and you could imagine hearing birds screech and animals roar.

I wonder if Elvis's hound dog chewed his Blue Suede Shoes?

I was really sorry that I missed out on the next adventure. A very famous hotel in Memphis, The Peabody, is known for housing ducks in their penthouse. It has an elegant lobby with ornate furnishings and lovely bouquets

of flowers. In the center of the lobby is a fountain. It looks like a big wishing well. Every morning the ducks come down to the lobby, where they spend the day swimming in the fountain.

The afternoon Mama C and Papa Pete were there, the lobby was packed with people waiting to see the parade. The Duckmaster went around and gave duck badges to many of the children in the crowd.

At 5:00 the Duckmaster rolled out a red carpet from the fountain to the elevator. He opened the elevator door and put the elevator on hold. Then he brought a step stool and put it next to the fountain.

Now, don't you think my presence would have added to the whole ceremony?

The Duckmaster walked over and tapped on the rim of the fountain. The ducks looked at him as if to say, do we have to get out? The ducks thought about it for a minute, then finally, one by one, got up on the rim of the fountain and proceeded down the steps. March music was playing as they slowly wad-dled along the red carpet to the elevator.

When all six ducks were on, the Duckmaster got on, closed the door, and they went up to the penthouse for the night.

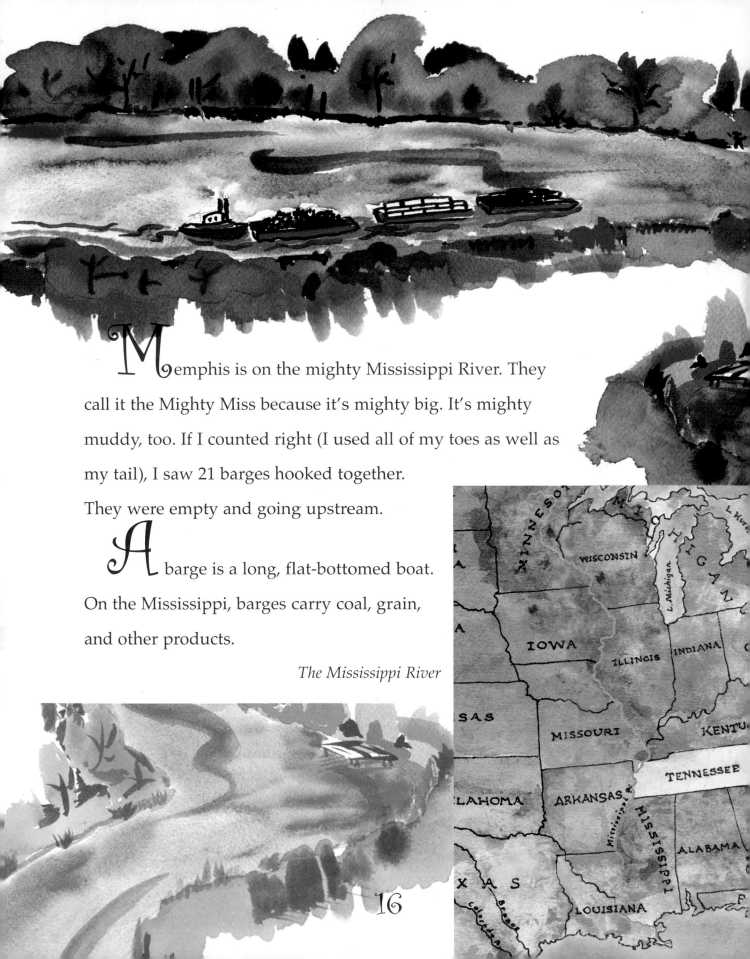

Memphis is on the mighty Mississippi River. They call it the Mighty Miss because it's mighty big. It's mighty muddy, too. If I counted right (I used all of my toes as well as my tail), I saw 21 barges hooked together. They were empty and going upstream.

A barge is a long, flat-bottomed boat. On the Mississippi, barges carry coal, grain, and other products.

The Mississippi River

16

run through and wallow in. Since I'm a chocolate lab, no one would have realized that I had been in the mud. Then again they might have, and that would have meant a bath.

My folks enjoyed seeing Little Rock, Arkansas. It's the state's largest city as well as the capital. They were sorry that it wasn't time for the roses to be blooming because Little Rock is

Greetings from Arkansas!

known as the "City of Roses." I was glad when they were through looking. I don't like city driving, stop and go — stop and go. I like smooth country driving.

After we crossed the Mississippi River into Arkansas, the land was quite flat. . . in fact, it was all mud flats. Those mud flats would have been fun to

Across the Prairie Plains

After all of that sightseeing, I was really tired. I took a long nap, and when I woke up, we were already in Oklahoma. Papa Pete and Mama C were talking about the Butterfield Overland Mail Route. That was the fastest way to get mail across the country in the mid-1800s. It ran from St. Louis to San Francisco, and even though the stage coaches traveled 24 hours a day, it still took 25 days to complete the route!

Inside the coach there were three seats that pulled out flat for sleeping. Sometimes they had six to ten passengers sleeping in that area. The stage coaches traveled through heat, dust, mud, rain, snow and wind. The ride was rough. Compared with that, traveling alone in the back seat of our car with my toys and bed seemed pretty comfy.

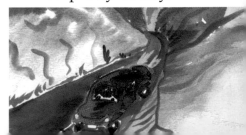

Then Mama C and Poppa Pete started talking about the Chisholm Trail and cowboys. Cowboys? My ears perked up. Mama C said that in the mid-1800s, cowboys in Texas drove their herds of cattle along the Chisholm Trail through Oklahoma to Kansas, where they were shipped east by rail. Over time, some cowboys realized that Oklahoma was not only closer to the railroad, it also had good grazing land. So, many cowboys chose to have a cattle ranch in Oklahoma. In Oklahoma City, the capital, my folks stopped to see the National Cowboy and Western Heritage Museum.

This complex is a national memorial to the men and women who pioneered the West. There are 20 areas to the museum, telling and showing you about the cowboys, Native Americans, and the pioneer life. They even have a children's wing where you can learn all kinds of things about life in the Old West.

My folks said it was most impressive to see. As usual, I didn't get to go in. Now, I'm sure those pioneers had dogs with them! (And so did the Native Americans!)

NEW MEXICO

OKLAHOMA

ARKANSAS

LOUISIANA

MEXICO

Wе were in Texas for only a short time because we were driving through the Texas Panhandle. It's called a panhandle because it is a narrow strip of land projecting like a handle between two states.

Texas

I saw many oil wells in Texas, but only some of them were pumping. The arm on the pump had a slow, steady action, up and down, up and down.

I was getting hungry. Many of the men in the trucks we passed were wearing cowboy hats, and I bet those wide brims would be real tasty.

ZZZ-ZZZZ-ZZZ-ZZ-Z-ZZZ-Z-ZZZ-ZZZ-ZZZZ

20

Our first stop was Palo Duro Canyon State Park, just below Amarillo, Texas. The Red River has carved spires and pinnacles, and some of the walls plunge a thousand feet to the canyon floor.

I had never seen terrain like this. Instead of being speechless, I was barkless in awe of the beauty. Now I knew that I was getting to a different part of the country.

Just west of Amarillo, we went by the Cadillac Ranch. I'd been waiting a long time to see a ranch, but this was not what I expected a ranch to look like. This ranch has ten Cadillacs buried nose deep in a field. This is a strange western ranch, I thought. I still scratch my head every time I think about it.

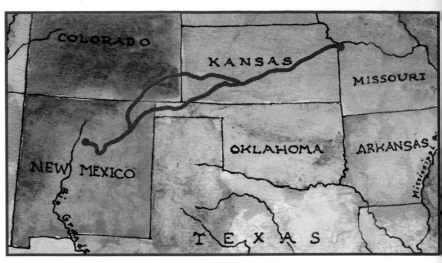

Old Santa Fe Trail

Next we were on our way up to Colorado. Trinidad, the first town we saw in Colorado, is known as the Gateway to the Rockies. Trinidad is on the Old Santa Fe Trail and was a supply center for settlers and traders traveling both west and east many years ago.

The Old Santa Fe Trail was very important to our western history. Before the railroads, the Trail was the only route from Independence, Missouri, to Santa Fe, New Mexico.

Lucy's journey

Finally we got to Craig's house in Colorado. I didn't realize that Craig's family was going to keep me on the alert all the time. Craig had a one-year old son, a four-month-old puppy, and a big black cat. The baby bounced on me, the puppy barked at me, and the cat hissed at me. It was enough to wear anyone out!

22

I was relieved when we left on the last stretch of our trip. Steve lives in Santa Fe, and we were going to stay with him until my folks found a house there. I must say that I pretty much slept the entire trip from Colorado to New Mexico because I was so tired.

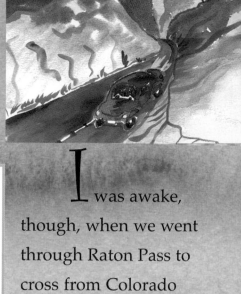

I was awake, though, when we went through Raton Pass to cross from Colorado into New Mexico. Raton Pass was a particularly difficult crossing in the mountain branch of the Old Santa Fe Trail. Just going through Raton Pass could take seven days back then!

In 1866 some mountain men cleared 27 miles of the mountainous terrain to make a road through Raton Pass. They set up a tollgate and charged $1.50 per wagon to go over it. That was a lot of money back then. Now the road is an interstate highway.

Today, more than a hundred years later, deep swales (ruts) can still be seen along the Trail. Rainwater runs in the ruts and erodes them. Some swales are as deep as 4 to 5 feet and 10 to 12 feet wide. That's as wide as some rooms.

The Wild West

From the moment we drove into Santa Fe, I knew it was a doggy town. Almost every car and truck had a big dog in it, wagging its tail. There weren't too many houses, but there was lots of open space and hills for running. The hills are covered with junipers and pinons.

I wanted to explore this Santa Fe that was in the Wild West. So about three minutes after we arrived at Steve's house, I went tearing out of the door.

I ran all over. I had a great time sniffing the new smells of the pines and dirt. Pretty soon I ran into several dogs and decided to stay with them for a while.

Jackrabbits have long hind legs and very tall ears.

The pinon is a low pine with large, edible seeds called "pine nuts."

Coyotes are wild members of the canine species.

In the meantime, my folks had been walking, driving, calling, and looking for me. Papa Pete even got lost in the pines. Finally he found himself and, eventually, me.

Two little dogs lived near Steve's house, and we became friends. I really had a good time with Chica and Tinker. We liked to go for walks, particularly in the snow.

There was always the possibility that we would see a jackrabbit. Tinker and Chica would look in drainage pipes to see if any jackrabbits were hiding in them.

It wasn't unusual to hear coyotes howling at night. Sometimes the coyotes sounded very close, and the mournful sound of their howling gave me the chills. That sound made me think that I must really be in the Wild West.

An adobe house has a tan, clay appearance, because adobe is made of mud and straw. Most houses have vigas, which are logs in the ceiling that go through the wall and extend outside about 12 to 18 inches. The roofs are flat. A lot of adobe homes have adobe walls around them to give people greater privacy.

25

In 1609, a Spanish colony moved to be near a little stream at the foot of the Sangre de Cristo mountain chain. Legend says that the native peoples had called this place "the place of the dancing ground of the sun," but because the governor lived there, the Spanish called it La Villa Real de Santa Fe de San Francisco de Asis (the Royal City of Holy Faith of Saint Francis of Assisi). By late 1610, Santa Fe had a large central Plaza, a fonda (inn), and government offices in the Palace of the Governors. Santa Fe has the oldest continuous seat of government in the United States—almost 400 years. Just think how many dog years that would be!

The Santa Fe Trail ends at the Plaza, but there the Trail links with the Old Spanish Trail to Los Angeles, California, and El Camino Real (the Royal Road) to Mexico City, Mexico. So, it is not surprising that the Plaza has been the meeting place for locals and visitors for many, many years.

In the daytime, the Plaza is full of people walking, chatting, and looking at the arts and crafts for sale in front of the Palace of the Governors. Native Americans sit in the shade of the portal and spread their jewelry and pottery on a blanket for people to view and buy.

Old Spanish Trail

One night, my folks were invited to visit someone, and I went along. This was a new location for me, and I wanted to explore more of Santa Fe. After we had been in the house for a while, I went out the dog door, squeezed through the gate, and took off like a race horse. New hills, new pinons, new dogs and cats — I ran and ran. Naturally, I did not know my way back, so I just kept running.

As the night got colder, I realized I was tired and hungry. I went down into an arroyo and curled up in a carved-out bank, not feeling too happy. Maybe exploring by myself wasn't the best idea.

An arroyo is the dry bed of a stream or river, like a gully.

28

In the morning, I still didn't know where I was. I was even colder and hungrier, and it was starting to snow. How would I ever find my folks? How would they ever find me?

29

My folks and Steve had driven around looking for me until midnight. By 6:00 in the morning, they were out again, looking and calling for me. By now, though, I was three miles away, near the Plaza. It was snowing quite hard, and they would have had trouble even spotting me because of the poor visibility. After much searching, they went home very dejected.

They called the local dog authorities and just hoped. With so much open space, they were very worried that no one would ever find me.

But a very nice man who was walking his dogs in the early morning noticed me, and realized that I seemed to be lost. He took me home, fed me, and gave me a warm place to lie down.

That nice gentleman made many calls to find my folks' temporary Santa Fe address. Thanks to his efforts, I was back with my family that day. Steve was the first one I saw, and I could hardly contain myself. I wagged my tail and licked his face. I was so happy and relieved to be back with my folks.

At last our house was ready, and we moved in. Unlike our condo in North Carolina, this house was right on the ground, and it had a fenced yard. I could go in and out of the house any time I pleased. That was really nice because I could quickly check out any rabbits in my yard. But, the lizards were too swift for me.

I wasn't expecting a new food treat in Santa Fe, and at first I had to beg and beg to get it. Do you know what a biscochito is? It is New Mexico's state cookie, and it is yummy. Now every once in a while I get to have one of those instead of a dog biscuit.

Recipe for Biscochitos

2 cups lard, vegetable shortening, or butter
1 1/2 cups sugar
2 eggs
2 tsp. toasted anise seeds
6 cups flour
3 tsp. baking powder
1 tsp. salt
1/2 cup brandy
TOPPING: 1/2 cup sugar, 1 tsp. cinnamon

Preheat oven to 350°. Cream the shortening, add eggs, sugar, and anise seeds and cream again. Mix dry ingredients separately and combine with the egg mixture. Add brandy and mix thoroughly. Roll the dough out on a floured surface and cut into desired shapes. Sprinkle with cinnamon/sugar topping and bake for 12 to 15 minutes until lightly browned.

Can you believe it? My folks were right! I've made new dog friends. I like watching the animals. I like looking at the mountains and the brilliant stars at night. And, the sky here usually has big puffy clouds in the daytime. They look so soft that I bet they would make a good place to nap.

I really like living in New Mexico in the Wild West. I'm converted—I'm a Western dog now!

The End

Lucy

The author, Charlotte Piepmeier, has
lived in 5 other states and now enjoys
living in Santa Fe, New Mexico.

The illustrator, Sally Blakemore, loves
dogs more than any species on earth.
She lives in Santa Fe, New Mexico
with her husband Rusty, their three
dogs, two naked rats, two birds, and
two fish. Although she was born in
Texas, she has lived in Washington,
D.C., New York City, New Orleans,
and Santa Fe.

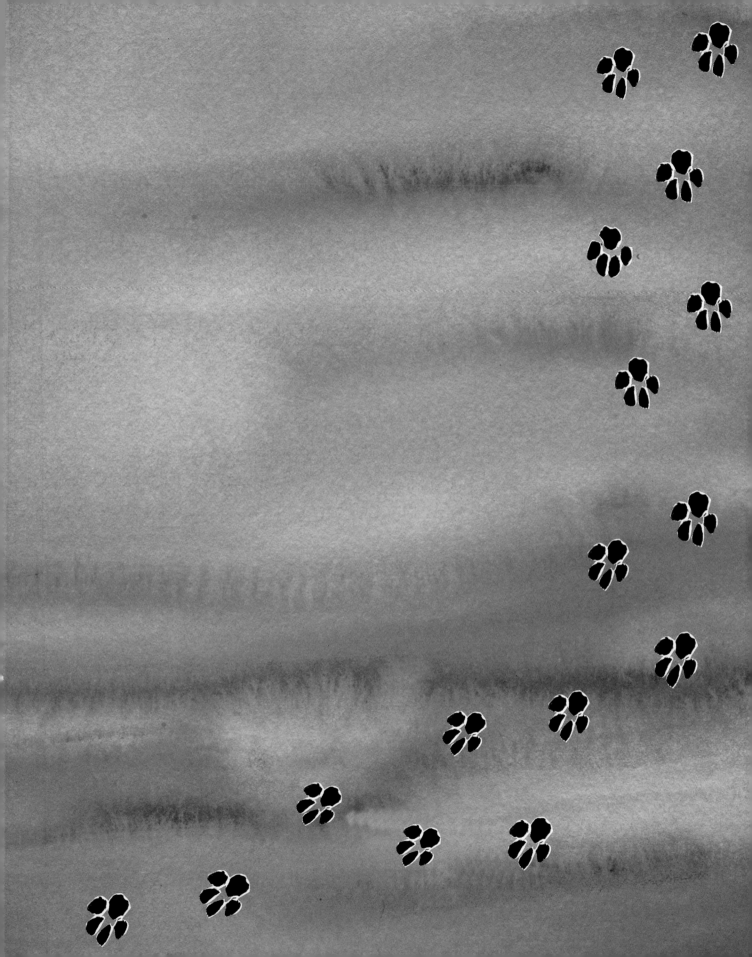

PACIFIC OCEAN

C A N

WASHINGTON

MONTANA

Missouri R.

NORTH DAKOTA

Yellowstone R.

IDAHO

OREGON

WYOMING

SOUTH DAKOT

CALIFORNIA

NEVADA

NEBRASK

UTAH

COLORADO

Pueblo

KAN

Trinidad

Raton

ARIZONA

Santa Fe

NEW MEXICO

OK

Rio Grande

TE

ICO

LUCY'S JOURNEY